This Is Your Garden

soil

trowel

seeds

water

light

time

coneflower

poppy

zinnia

pincushion flower

seedlings

weeds

rain

pansy

impatiens

bellflower

petunia

cosmos

delphinium

This Is Your Garden

Maggie Smith

Dragonfly Books® New York

This is your garden.
It is yours and yours alone.
It is yours for keeps.

These are the things you will need
    for your garden:
    your own space for planting,
    good tools,
    and seeds.

Some seeds you may get from
    your friends and family.
Some you will find in the backyard.

Others you will find
inside your own pocket.

First, make a nice soft bed in the ground.
Dig the warm soil and take out any big stones.

Scatter the seeds,
   or place them in rows.

Then cover them up with a blanket of earth.

Now they'll need water and sun,
   light and time.
You can tell them a story
   or sing them a song of encouragement.

   Soon tiny seedlings
         will poke up their heads
               to see what's going on
                     out there.

They will be very delicate at first,
    so you will need to protect them.
Pull up any weeds
    that try to crowd them out.

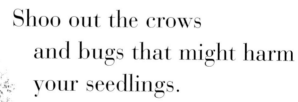

Shoo out the crows
and bugs that might harm
your seedlings.

As the little plants grow,
  some will be straight
  and some will be wobbly.
Some might be thirstier than others.

But they will all need you.

This is your garden.

There will be days
when it's dark and rainy
and you can't tend to your garden.

You can stay inside with
your favorite book,

and know that your garden
is getting a good soaking.

But sometimes, even if it's sunny,
    you may wander through other gardens
    to see what's growing there.

In some gardens a quick peek is enough.

But in others you could stay all day.
They may have flowers
    you want to grow in your garden too.

Your garden will wait for you,
and it will always
be happy to see you
when you return.

As your garden grows fuller,
 you may need to thin some things out.
You can kiss them good-bye
 and say you'll visit on Thursdays.

Now there is room
for the old plants to flourish

and space to add
something
new.

If you think that your garden
is not growing fast enough,
do not worry.

Give it plenty of water,
let the light shine—
and your garden will grow…

...in its own perfect time.

For Jessica

Happy growing!

Published by
Dragonfly Books®
an imprint of
Random House Children's Books
a division of Random House, Inc.
1540 Broadway
New York, New York 10036

Visit us on the Web! www.randomhouse.com/kids

Educators and librarians, for a variety of teaching tools, visit us at
www.randomhouse.com/teachers

Library of Congress Cataloging-in-Publication Data
Smith, Maggie.
  This is your garden / Maggie Smith.
    p. cm.
  Summary: A little girl, given good tools and seeds, begins to grow a garden that needs water, sun,
weeding, and her encouragement.
  ISBN: 0-517-70992-9 (trade)   0-517-70993-7 (lib. bdg.)   0-440-41736-8 (pbk.)
  1. Gardening—Juvenile literature. [1. Gardening.] I. Title.
  SB457.S68   1998   97-31963
  635—dc21

Reprinted by arrangement with Crown Publishers
Printed in the United States of America
April 2001
10 9 8 7 6 5 4 3 2 1

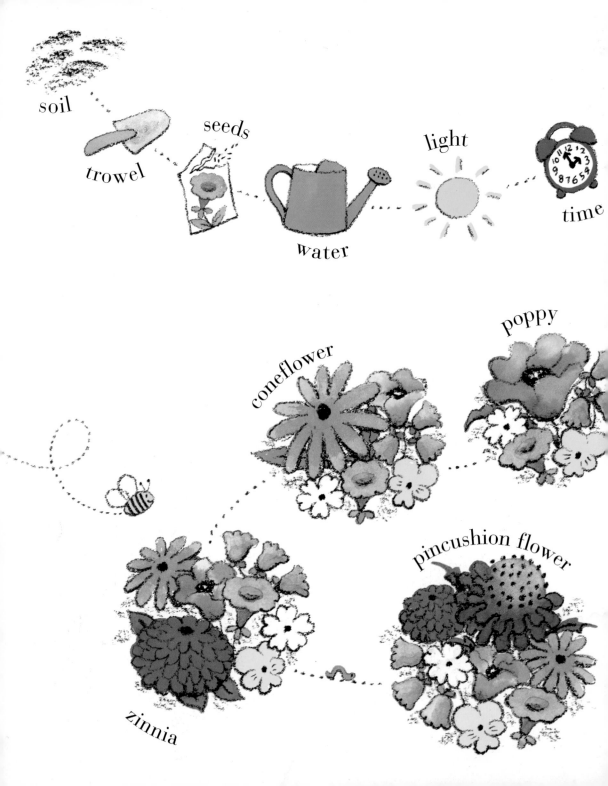

soil

trowel

seeds

water

light

time

coneflower

poppy

pincushion flower

zinnia

seedlings

weeds

rain

pansy

impatiens

bellflower

petunia

cosmos

delphinium